BEAST

Friends Forever

Book 2

THE SUPER
SWAP-O SUPRISE!

Nate Evans and Vince Evans

sourcebooks
jabberwocky

Copyright © 2011 by Nate Evans and Vince Evans
Cover and internal illustrations © Nate Evans and Vince Evans
Cover and internal design © 2011 by Sourcebooks, Inc.
Series design by Liz Demeter/Demeter Design
Sourcebooks and the colophon are registered trademarks of Sourcebooks, Inc.

The characters and events portrayed in this book are fictitious or are used
fictitiously. Any similarity to real persons, living or dead, is purely coincidental
and not intended by the author.

Published by Sourcebooks Jabberwocky, an imprint of Sourcebooks, Inc.
P.O. Box 4410, Naperville, Illinois 60567-4410
(630) 961-3900
Fax: (630) 961-2168
www.jabberwockykids.com

Library of Congress Cataloging-in-Publication data is on file with the publisher.

Source of Production: Versa Press, East Peoria, Illinois, USA
Date of Production: June 2011
Run Number: 15436

Printed and bound in the United States of America.
VP 10 9 8 7 6 5 4 3 2 1

To all the wonderful doctors, nurses, and staff
at Mayo Clinic in Jacksonville and Summit
Cancer Care in Statesboro.
Thank you so much for your kindness
and excellent care for my wife. You changed
our lives in profound ways.
—Nate

For Nate,
My brother and friend
—Vince

CONTENTS

WELCOME TO TRIPSEN FALLS

TOP SECRET!!!

THIS NOTEBOOK IS GUARDED BY MAN-EATING CROCODILES!!

Keep Away!

Grrr!

My name is Zeke Bird. My sister is named Hannah (but sometimes I call her banana brain).

One day, me and Hannah went monster hunting, and GUESS WHAT!! We caught a real monster! He was hiding under my bed. His name is Otto. He's green and hairy and kind of goofy.

Hoobah!

Yay! Me so great!

OTTO

by Zeke

Otto is not even a little scary, which is too bad because I have all kinds of big, stinky bully problems at school.

P. U.

Sid the squid!

Otto got to my house by stowing away in a big box of candy that my dad sent. My dad is in the navy and travels all over the world on a huge aircraft carrier!

JETS ARE COOL

DAD's Aircraft carrier

Otto in the box

To Zeke

by Zeke

Otto comes from a mysterious place called
Triangle Island. All kinds of weird stuff lives
there, like monsters and pirates and dinosaurs! Otto ran away when evil trolls took
over. I guess Otto had big bully problems
too. He doesn't have big muscles or claws or

anything like that. But even if Otto isn't so tough, he is still amazing! He has magic powers! He can change his size and do swap-o tricksy tricks! That's really TOP SECRET!!

POOF!

MAGIC

by Zeke

small Otto

Big Otto

Otto lives with us now—except my mom doesn't know it. Otto says we're going to have lots of awesome adventures! He says I better wear clean underwear! Ha ha! But I'm tough enough to handle anything...I hope...

CHAPTER 1

Blast Off?

"Get ready for countdown!" Zeke Bird said, adjusting his goggles. "I'm going to blast off on a dragon!"

"Ha ha, you'll blast all right," said his sister, Hannah. "'Cause the last time you flew on a dragon, you barfed all over our school."

Hannah twirled on one foot and sang:
"Fish-head stew is raining down,
Zeke launched his lunch all over town.
You better run. You better hide.
When Zeke goes for a dragon ride."

"I didn't barf," grumbled Zeke. But he had to admit it had been a close call. This time would be better.

It was Saturday morning, and Zeke was out in the backyard with Hannah and their new BFF (Beast Friend Forever) named Otto. Otto could do amazing things. A few days before,

he'd magically traded one of Zeke's drawings for an awesome, fiery, farting dragon. Zeke had zoomed through the sky on the dragon. It had been like riding a crazy flying roller coaster. Then POOF! The dragon had disappeared. Now Zeke wanted to ride that dragon again.

Zeke opened his sketchbook. "Where's that rocket sketch?" he muttered, flipping past his drawings of airplanes and fighter jets.

"Hurry up and swap-o something already," Hannah said to Zeke. "You're hogging the magic. Right, Otto?"

"Not magic," said Otto. "Tricksy tricks. Wahooo!" Riding one of Zeke's toy planes like a skateboard, the little beast zipped around Hannah's foot.

"Pipe down, banana brain," said Zeke, glaring at his sister. "We have to learn how swap-o works."

"Boring," said Hannah. "Just ask Otto."

"Me not know how swap-o works," said the beast. "Me can just do it. Wheee!" His jet skateboard slammed into Zeke's sneaker. Otto tumbled through the air, and crashed headfirst

into the sandbox. "Blargh!" said Otto, spitting out globs of sand. "Me eat a *sand*wich!"

"Good one," said Zeke.

"How come you think Otto's jokes are funny but not mine," asked Hannah.

"Because the only thing funny about you is your face," said Zeke, grinning.

"Oh yeah?" said Hannah. "The only funny thing about you is your butt!"

Zeke laughed. "Okay, here's what we know about swap-o. When Otto says his magic word, *hoobah*—"

"Best word ever," said Otto.

"That makes a swap-o happen," said Zeke. "And a swap-o trades something here for something on Triangle Island."

"Like when Otto swapped our swing set for a goofy giraffe," said Hannah. "And you fell off."

"I did not fall off," said Zeke.

"And then," Hannah said, "Otto swapped your drawing for a stinky dragon!"

"Yay!" said Otto. "Me save you from troll-boy!"

"Sid Slamburg," grumbled Zeke. "That creep almost ruined everything."

Sid Slamburg was a bully who always picked on Zeke. He was as big as a pro wrestler and looked like he ate nothing but raw meat.

"Sid's a booger brain," said Hannah.

"Sid go SPLAT!" shouted Otto happily. Sid and Zeke had both ended up riding the wild dragon. But Sid had slipped off, crash-landing into a herd of hamsters.

Zeke grinned, remembering the look of crazy panic on the bully's face as he fled from the furious fur balls.

"But that dragon didn't stick around very long," said Zeke. "Otto's swap-os only last for a few minutes. And there's tons of other stuff about swap-o we have to figure out. We gotta be like real scientists. We have to observe stuff and measure things." Zeke pointed at a collection of objects scattered around him. "So I got my notebook, my sketchbook, my watch, my camera, my ruler, my calculator, my helmet, and some oven mitts so I can handle that dragon."

"Me got a cookie," said Otto.

"Let's measure it," said Hannah.

"Get serious," said Zeke. "Hey, here it is!" He slapped his sketchbook. "This is the drawing Otto swapped out for that awesome rocket-dragon! Okay, Otto, you ready?"

"Lookie, no more cookie," said Otto sadly.

"Come on," said Zeke. "Do the rocket swap-o like you did before."

"Aye, aye," hollered the little beast. He scrunched up his face, thinking hard, then tapped Zeke's drawing of a rocket and shouted, "Hoobah!"

There was a bright flash of green light, and the sketchbook vanished.

POOF!

In its place was a big, weird metal object. The surface of the object was battered and burned. It looked old, and there was a strange, faded symbol painted on its side.

"Blast off?" said Otto.

"That's not a dragon," Zeke said, pulling off his helmet and goggles.

"Duh," said Hannah. "So what is it?"

"Big lunch box?" said Otto hopefully.

"I think it's some kind of spaceship," said Zeke.

"Maybe there's an alien inside," Hannah said. "A green, slimy alien monster!"

There was a CLUNK! from inside the ship.

"Eeep!" shrieked Hannah.

A hatch popped opened.

"Yowee!" cried Otto. "Haul anchor!" The tiny beast scampered up Zeke's leg, then clung to his shoulder like a pirate's parrot.

Slowly, something crawled out the ship's hatch…

Something smelly and hunchbacked…

Something with a huge head and long arms…

Something that wasn't human!

Then the thing reached up *and pulled off its head!*

CHAPTER 2

One Banana, Two Banana

"Gross!" gasped Hannah.

"Gah!" Zeke cried. "Oh wait…that's just a helmet."

Now they could see the creature's face.

"It's…a monkey," said Hannah.

"In a space suit," said Zeke. "I bet that's an old rocket from when they used to blast monkeys into space. It must have crash-landed on Triangle Island!"

"So you got a funky monkey instead of the rocket-dragon?" asked Hannah.

"Sometimes swap-o not get what me want," Otto said with a sigh.

"Bummer," said Zeke.

The monkey scowled at them. It started jumping up and down, shaking its fist.

"Ook, ook," shrieked the monkey.

"I don't think it's happy to see us," said Zeke.

"What should we do?" asked Hannah.

Otto jumped up and down on Zeke's shoulder.

"Ook, ook," shouted Otto.

"What did you say?" Zeke asked.

"Don't know," said Otto. "Me not speak monkey."

"Oh great," muttered Zeke.

"Do something, Mr. Big Shot Scientist!" said Hannah.

"Yeah…right," said Zeke, reaching slowly for his camera. He pointed it at the monkey and clicked the button. The flash popped like lightning.

The monkey shrieked in surprise and fell over. Then, snarling and flapping its slobbery lips, the creature reached into the rocket and yanked out a big bunch of bananas.

"Maybe it wants to have a picnic," said Hannah.

Waving the bananas in the air, the monkey screeched, "Kreegah!"

There was a bright flash of yellow light.

POOF! The bunch of bananas popped apart.

"Oooh," said Otto. "Monkey has tricksy tricks!"

Instead of just lying there, looking ripe and good to eat, the bananas were now hopping wildly about on little legs. They were hooting and yipping. Their yellow faces were streaked with colorful war paint.

"You gotta be kidding me," said Zeke.

"Whoo hoo," said Otto. "Good trick!"

Hannah squinted at the bananas. "What are they holding?" she asked.

"Spears," Zeke said with a gulp. "And axes and boomerangs!"

"Ook, ook!" screeched the monkey in the space suit, pointing.

The little banana warriors turned and glared at Zeke and Hannah.

"Kong!" growled the monkey.

"KOOONNNGGG!!" howled the savage bananas.

And then they charged…

CHAPTER 3

Food Fight!

CHAPTER 4

If You Love Bananas So Much, Why Don't You Marry One?

Fighting off three banana barbarians, Zeke stared in horror as his mom opened the back door.

When suddenly...

POOF!

In a flash of green light, the angry chimp and the battered rocket vanished. Zeke's sketchbook plopped onto the grass.

POOF! There was a flash of yellow light. The little banana savages transformed back into harmless fruit and tumbled to the ground.

"Yipe!" Otto dove inside Zeke's backpack, as Zeke's mom said, "Sounds like feeding time at the zoo out here."

Mom stepped onto the patio, then stopped

in surprise. "What are you doing with all these bananas?"

"Uh…it's homework," said Zeke.

"We're playing Banana Bingo Bongo," said Hannah at the same time.

"For, um, you know…school," mumbled Zeke.

Mom raised an eyebrow. "Well, dial down the volume on the Bongo, all right?" She went back inside.

"You're lousy at excuses," Hannah said to Zeke.

Zeke sighed. "We're just lucky a wild banana didn't poke Mom with a spear. Otto's swap-o ended just in time. I guess when the monkey vanished, his magic did too."

Otto scrambled out of the backpack. "Bye-bye, monkey-face," called the little beast.

"So if that was just some regular old space-monkey," Hannah said, "how come it can do magic?"

"Because it crash-landed on Triangle Island," said Zeke.

"Everyone on island has tricksy tricks," said Otto.

"Yeah," said Zeke. "Otto told me that anyone who lives on the island gets a magic power. Like, Otto can do swap-o. That monkey can bring bananas to life—"

"I want a magic power too!" said Hannah.

"Abracadabra! Boppity boo!
Think of all the things I'd do.
Change Zeke to a big pink duck,
Sell him for a million bucks!"

28

Zeke rolled his eyes. "Like I was saying," he continued, "you gotta be on Triangle Island. And we can't get there."

"No go!" growled Otto. "Trolls there!"

"It's weird, though," said Zeke. "Otto's swap-o ended, and the monkey disappeared, but lots of bananas stuck around. I wonder why? Maybe some bananas were too far away from the monkey or something, and they didn't go back with him…"

Zeke's sentence dribbled to a stop. His mouth just hung open, as he stared at Otto. The little beast had scampered over and picked up a banana.

"Banana try to hurt me. Now me hurt banana!" said Otto happily. Then he chomped into the ripe yellow fruit.

"Gross," screeched Hannah. "You gotta peel it first."

"Holy cow!" shouted Zeke. He snatched the banana from Otto. "HOLY COW!"

"What's the big deal?" asked Hannah. "It's a banana."

"Gimme!" Otto jumped up and down, trying to grab the fruit back from Zeke.

"Don't you get it!?" cried Zeke, shaking the banana wildly in the air.

"What?" asked Hannah.

"This banana," said Zeke, *"is from Triangle Island!"*

"So what," said Hannah.

Otto scrambled up onto Zeke's outstretched

arm, then made a flying leap at the banana. He clamped onto it with his teeth.

"So the *monkey* brought the *bananas*," said Zeke, getting more and more excited. "*And the bananas stayed here, even after the monkey and the rocket disappeared!*"

"I didn't know you liked bananas so much," said Hannah. "Maybe that's why you smell like a monkey."

Zeke dropped Otto and the banana, snatched up a pencil, and started scribbling in his notebook. The notebook was labeled TOP SECRET in big block letters across the front.

"This is the most amazing discovery ever!" cried Zeke. "*We can keep stuff from Triangle Island!* Not just bananas. There are lots of cool things on the island! Like dinosaurs! And pirates!"

"Yo ho ho," said Otto, his mouth crammed with banana.

"So maybe we can get something awesome and keep it," said Zeke. "Like a dinosaur egg! Or some buried treasure! Or—"

"Or some dino poop!" cried Hannah.

"There's still a lot we have to figure out," said Zeke. His eyes sparkled with energy. "The Super Swap-O Experiment is just getting started!"

"Blast off!" said Otto.

CHAPTER 5

When You Gotta Go

"Get in the backpack, Otto," said Zeke. "We got places to go!"

"Roger dodger," said the beast, diving inside the pack.

Zeke picked it up and raced into the house. Hannah was right behind him. "Where are we going?" she asked.

Zeke bounded up the stairs to his room.

"Just grab a bunch of stuff," said Zeke, pulling a big beat-up duffel bag from his closet. "Whatever we can fit in this."

"What kind of stuff?" Hannah asked.

"Stuff for Otto to trade," said Zeke. He snatched some toys off the floor and tossed them into the duffel.

Hannah rushed to her bedroom. "Wait for me," she called.

Zeke scooped up anything that looked interesting. Shoving an old combat boot into the duffel bag, he muttered, "Wow, Dad sure has big feet."

Zeke's dad was a jet mechanic on an aircraft carrier. It was a super-important job, but it also meant his dad was away from home a lot. Zeke sighed. There was definitely a Dad-shaped hole in his life.

Hannah burst back into the room, her arms loaded with dolls, toys, and costumes. She squeezed everything into Zeke's duffel bag.

"Now what?" she asked breathlessly.

"Mom," shouted Zeke, struggling to close the bulging bag. "We need to go to the park! To do some homework!"

"Homework?" Hannah groaned, rolling her eyes.

Zeke carefully slung his backpack with Otto still inside over one shoulder. Then he said, "Help me lift," and picked up one end of the duffel bag. Hannah grabbed the other end and they half-dragged, half-carried the lumpy, bumpy bag downstairs.

"I can't take you to the park right now," Mom called from her office. "I need to finish this report."

"But this is really superduper, mega-important," said Hannah. "'Cause if Zeke can't get to the park, then he's gonna flunk fourth grade. He might even get flunked back to second grade and be in my class and he'll be so embarrassed he'll never get over it! He'll grow up to be a real loser, begging for cookies at the bus stop!"

Hannah smiled and flashed Zeke a quick thumbs up.

Zeke frowned.

There was a muffled giggle from Zeke's backpack.

Mom sighed, and picked up the phone. "Let me see if Mrs. McQueen is free…"

"Yay!" said Hannah.

Oh no! thought Zeke. *Not her!*

CHAPTER 6

The Babysitter

Five minutes later, Zeke, Hannah, Otto, and the heavy duffel bag were out on the sidewalk, waiting.

"So, what are we doing?" asked Hannah. "And why do I have to carry these bananas?"

"It's too dangerous to do swap-o experiments at home," said Zeke. "Mom almost saw those killer bananas."

Otto giggled. "Killer bananas," he said. "Yum!"

"So we're going to the park to do our experiments," Zeke said. "And we can't leave those bananas here. What if they come back to life and attack Mom?" He glanced down the street searching for the dreaded purple car. "Otto, you have to get in my backpack and be quiet till we get to the park."

"Aye, aye, captain," said Otto, jumping into the pack.

Zeke and Hannah heard the radio blasting music before they saw the car.

With a loud rattle and a cough of black exhaust, a huge purple station wagon pulled up beside them. Weathered wooden panels decorated the side of the car. A rainbow-colored surfboard was jammed on the roof rack.

The passenger door popped open.

"Hi, Mrs. McQueen!" Hannah shouted over the thundering music.

A small, wrinkled old woman with

bubble-gum pink hair and yellow sunglasses
sat behind the steering wheel. Her bright
polka-dotted bathing suit matched the color
of her hair. She grinned and waved, then
hollered, "Climb aboard, Hannah! I like you!
You got loads of moxie!"

"What's moxie?" Hannah asked.

"It means you got fighting spirit," said Mrs. McQueen. "Just like me in the old days! I was working on a sardine boat and we got jumped by an ornery giant squid. Ha, we showed that slimy sea-chicken a thing or two!"

Zeke managed to heave the duffel bag into the backseat. Then he climbed up on the fuzzy lime-green front seat beside Hannah and the bag of bananas.

Mrs. McQueen stared at Zeke. "Ahoy, boy! Yer lookin' a little scrawny. You need to eat more sardines!"

"Ugh," Zeke mumbled.

"Squishy fishy!" cried Otto from Zeke's pack. But only Zeke heard him.

"Buckle up, you grunts!" shouted Mrs. McQueen.

Zeke and Hannah rammed their seat belts in place.

"Fire torpedoes!" yelled Mrs. McQueen. The old woman stomped down on the gas pedal and the car rocketed forward.

Hannah and Mrs. McQueen started singing

loudly along with the booming marching band music:

"Everywhere we go,
People wanna know,
Who we are!
So we tell them…"

"This is embarrassing," mumbled Zeke. He scrunched down as far as he could, hoping no one would see him. "But when I'm rich and famous it will all be worth it."

CHAPTER 7

Hannah's Turn

When the station wagon screeched to a stop at the park, Zeke jumped out and wrestled the duffel bag from the car. Hannah held the bag of bananas and Zeke's backpack carefully. "How you doing, Otto?" she whispered.

"Everywhere me go," sang Otto, his voice muffled by the backpack, "Pickles wanna know—"

"Okay, I hauled you grunts to the park," shouted Mrs. McQueen, glaring at Zeke and Hannah, "now you'll have to find your own way home. Here's a canteen and a Swiss Army Knife!" Then she cackled loudly. "I'm just teasin'." She pointed at a nearby bench. "I'm gonna read my surfing magazine right there. Come get me when you're ready to put an egg in your shoe and beat it."

"She's funny," said Hannah, giggling.

"Funny as a screen door on a submarine," muttered Zeke.

Zeke dragged the duffel behind a huge oak tree. Hannah skipped after him. Several nearby bushes guarded them from view, like large green linebackers protecting a quarterback. "We're okay here," said Zeke.

THE BIG KAHUNA

Heaving the duffel bag upside down, Zeke shook it roughly. Toy soldiers, dolls, spangled clothes, tattered books, and lots of other junk spilled onto the grass.

Unzipping Zeke's backpack, Hannah set it down near the tree. Otto popped up happily and looked out.

"Me sees trees in the breeze," he cried.

"Hand me my notebook and a pencil," said Zeke.

"Roger dodger," said the beast, grabbing the items from inside the backpack.

"Don't forget," said Hannah, "it's my turn for swap-o!"

"Okay, okay. Don't flip your pancake," said Zeke, scribbling in his top secret notebook. He looked at his watch. "Ready? GO!"

Hannah dug excitedly through the pile of odd objects from home.

"Swap-o this!" she cried, holding up a battered gold music box. "This, this, this!" All that was left of the little ballerina that had once twirled on top of the box was a plastic leg and a ragged tuft of pink tutu.

44

Hannah held the music box out to Otto. "Get me something good!"

"For Hannah Banana," cried the beast. Then he smacked the music box and squeaked, "Hoobah!"

There was a flash of bright green light…

CHAPTER 8

Bling-a-ding-ding!

POOF!

"Ooooh," gasped Hannah, staring in wonder.

"Let me see!" cried Zeke.

Clasped in Hannah's trembling hands was…

"Is it a bird?" whispered Hannah.

The creature looked like a bird, except its feathers were made of shiny solid gold. There was a key poking up from the bird's back.

"Is it a toy?" Zeke asked.

The bird's jeweled eyes blinked suddenly. Then the bird looked up at Hannah, opened its beak, and began to sing. The bird's whistle sounded like a strange, magical flute.

"HELLO BIRDY!" shouted Otto, waving cheerfully.

Squawking in fright, the bird rocketed into the air. As it flew up, a small golden blob plopped down into the grass.

"Yuck," said Zeke. "I think it pooped."

Hannah sat there, stunned.

Suddenly there was a flash of light.

POOF!

The golden bird was gone. Hannah's music box reappeared high in midair, hovered for a split-second, then crashed to the ground.

"Pretty cool," said Zeke, picking up his notebook.

"Omigosh!" said Hannah. "It's still here!"

"What?" Zeke asked.

"The bird poop," said Hannah. "*Only it's not poop!*" Kneeling in the grass, she carefully picked up the golden object.

Zeke scrambled to get a better look.

"It's an egg," Zeke said.

"Yum," said Otto.

"If you eat this, I'll eat you!" said Hannah sternly.

The egg was small and gold and perfect. It looked like it had been made by a fairy toy maker.

Zeke carefully took the golden object from his sister. He gasped. "These look real!" He pointed at some rubies, diamonds, and emeralds decorating the shiny shell. "Wow," he said, "this is a lot better than some freaky bananas. I bet this egg is worth a million dollars!"

Hannah grabbed the egg and held it to herself protectively. "I'm not going to sell it. I'm going to hatch it!" she said.

CHAPTER 9

Zeke's Turn

"Snack time," said Otto.

"Okay, sure," said Zeke. He fished a small box of raisins out of his pocket and handed it over.

"Whoo hoo!" cried Otto. The little beast gobbled most of the raisins, then shoved one up his nose. "Me save it for later!"

"So we've learned a few more things about swap-o," said Zeke. "Like, the things traded are the same in some ways. When Otto swapped your music box, you got a bird."

"Yeah," said Hannah. "The music box and the bird were both gold."

"And they both had wind-up keys and made music," said Zeke.

"Tooty flutey," said Otto.

"Sometimes the things traded are sort of the same, but different," said Zeke. "Like when Otto swapped my drawing of a rocket, he got a real rocket."

"Hooray!" said Otto. "It later now!" With a honk, he blasted the raisin out of his nose and into the air. It double-flipped just before Otto caught it in his mouth.

Hannah cried, "That is totally—"

"Dis-gus-ting!" groaned Zeke. "Okay, it's my turn for a swap-o trade."

"You'll never get anything better than this," said Hannah, pointing at her golden egg. "Just give up." She grinned, then started singing:

"I did a swap-o! Look what I got!
What did you get? Diddly-squat!"

"Oh yeah?" Zeke cried, interrupting her. "Well, I'm going to do the greatest swap-o ever!" He snatched up a dented, green robot. "*This* is a lot cooler than a dumb music box!" Holding the robot by the legs, Zeke thrust it at Otto. "Do it!"

"Aye, aye, captain!" said Otto. He tapped the robot. "Hoobah!"

There was a bright flash of light.

POOF!

The robot was gone.

And in its place was...

"Oh no!" cried Zeke. "*Not you!*"

CHAPTER 10

It's Not Easy Being Green

"Get yer paws off me!" shouted the little green man clutched in Zeke's hand. "Ya blasted bingo!"

"Gah!" said Zeke, dropping the small figure like he was a hot potato.

"It's the mean green goon," wailed Hannah.

The last time Zeke and Hannah had seen this tiny green tough guy was when Otto had swapped out one of Zeke's green toy dinosaurs. This little madman had magically appeared in its place. That time the green man had been taking a bath.

"Otto, what happened?" shouted Zeke. "He's not anything cool! Send him back!"

The little green man jumped up from where he'd fallen in the grass. "I'll teach you giants to mess with me!" he roared, shaking his fist at Zeke. "Bring yer nose down here so I can bop it!"

Suddenly, there was a loud rustling in the bushes behind them. A soccer ball came blasting out of the leaves. It bounced past Zeke and smacked into the little green man, knocking him on his butt.

"What the flamin' hoo-ha was that?" shouted the green man, spitting angrily. Then he saw the soccer ball rolling to a stop a few feet away. "A football?" he cried.

"That's not a football," said Hannah. "It's a soccer ball."

"What does a dumb giant know?" yelled the green man. "That's a football! And I can beat ya with one foot tied behind my back! Ya overgrown radish!"

With a howling yodel, the green man ran at the ball and kicked it with his tiny foot. The soccer ball rocketed toward Hannah's head. She ducked with a startled cry and the ball went whizzing past her into the bushes.

There was a loud BONK! and a "HEY!" from the other side of the shrubs.

"I can beat anyone!" shouted the green man. "No matter how big! Ya blasted radish!"

Then, with a flash of bright light and a POOF! the green man vanished. Zeke's little green robot was back.

At the same time, there were loud rustling and grunting sounds from the bushes.

A huge, horrible head pushed itself through the leaves.

"Who hit me?" growled the head.

Oh no! thought Zeke. *It's Sid the Squid!*

SMACK

CHAPTER 11

The Challenge

"Who hit *me* with *my* soccer ball?" asked Sid Slamburg, rubbing his forehead. He glared at Zeke.

Zeke took a step backward. From the corner of his eye, he saw Otto dive into the backpack.

"I should've known it was you, Birdbrain!" said Sid.

"N-no way," said Zeke.

"And you called me a radish!" yelled Sid. "You dork!"

"No, he didn't," cried Hannah. "Besides, you're not a radish. You're a stinky skunk cabbage!"

Sid whirled on Hannah. "Shut your pie-hole," he growled. "Hey, what's that?" With surprising speed, the bully snatched the golden egg away from Hannah.

"Give that back!" howled Hannah.

Sid held the egg high over his head. "You gonna cry, little baby?" he sneered.

"Just give it back," said Zeke.

"Hey," said Sid, "I heard you say that you could beat anyone at soccer!"

"That wasn't me," muttered Zeke.

Sid made a big show of looking around. "Well, I don't see anyone else here," said Sid. "Just Zeke the freak and his weirdo little sister."

"You stupid Slamburger buns," said Hannah.

"Hey," snarled Sid. "You want your dumb toy back? Then you gotta beat me at soccer!"

"Bring it on," yelled Hannah. "Zeke will kick your butt so bad you'll poop soccer balls for a week!"

Zeke heard a muffled giggle from inside his backpack.

Sid's face turned red. He shoved the golden egg into his pocket, then poked Zeke in the chest with a finger as big as a hotdog. "I'm gonna flatten you, freak! So let's get started..."

CHAPTER 12

A Man with a Plan

"I want to play too," said Hannah. She was following Sid and pulling Zeke along behind her. Zeke moved like a zombie. His legs felt rubbery. His stomach felt like he'd swallowed a can of squirmy worms.

"That's the plan," said Sid with a snicker. "If I gotta babysit my little cousin at least I can have some fun humiliating you dweebs while I do it."

They made their way to an open stretch of grass just beyond the bushes and the oak tree. There was a big kid standing there already. The closer they got, the bigger the kid looked.

Holy cow! That's Sid's little cousin? Zeke thought.

"Hey, Moronica!" said Sid. "These chumps think they can play soccer."

"Oh yeah?" asked Moronica, glaring at Zeke and Hannah. She was wearing a blue soccer uniform with yellow stars plastered on the front.

"This guy," said Sid, pointing at Zeke, "said he could kick our butts."

"This runt?" Moronica laughed like a snorting pig. "He couldn't kick his way out of a girl's bathroom." She glared at Zeke. "I'm the best soccer player in the whole peewee league! My team is called the Black Foot of Death!"

Zeke stared horrified at Moronica's one eyebrow. It crawled like a big furry caterpillar across her forehead. *And I think she's got fangs!* Zeke thought.

"We're not afraid of you," Hannah said. "Right, brother?"

How did this happen? Zeke wondered dismally. *But we have to get that gold egg back. I need a plan. I wish I were awesome and super-cool. I wish I were amazing at soccer…*

CHAPTER 13

Soccer Smack-Down!

"Oh, great," said Hannah, rolling her eyes. "They scored already! Didn't you hear me say go?"

"Guess not," said Zeke. With a sigh, he got up and brushed the grass off his pants. Sid and Moronica were cheering and slapping hands just beyond the tree that marked the goal on one side of the field.

"We have to win," said Hannah fiercely. "We have to get my egg back!"

Zeke watched as Sid and his cousin came swaggering back toward them.

"One to nothin'," said Sid, heaving the ball at Zeke. "Your ball, dork!"

Zeke quickly kicked the ball to Hannah, then ran upfield.

"Hyaah!" shouted Hannah, and booted the ball at Zeke. "Go, go, go!"

Sid and Moronica charged for the ball. Sid kicked out, tripping Zeke. As Zeke fought to stay on his feet, Moronica elbowed him in the stomach. He crashed to the ground.

Sid kicked the ball toward their goal, and Moronica charged at Hannah. Hannah tried to get the ball, but Moronica shoved her aside like an elephant swatting a fly.

"Goal for us!" Moronica shouted triumphantly. "Two to zip!"

The next ten minutes were some of the worst of Zeke's life. He was pounded and pummeled by Sid and his monster cousin. There was no referee, so the two big bullies were playing mean and dirty. Zeke had no chance to score, or even kick the ball. This was more like a ferocious gladiator battle than a soccer game.

Hannah was wheezing with frustration and her knee was bleeding.

"Eight to nothin'!" shouted Sid.

As Zeke spit out some grass and pushed himself up off the ground, he saw a flash of yellow over by the bushes. Otto was peeking out at them from behind some low branches. The little beast waved when he saw Zeke notice him.

Hannah stamped her foot and shouted at Sid, "You guys are big stinky cheaters!"

Sid and his cousin snickered. "We're just better than you," said Sid.

Hannah spun around and shouted at Zeke. "Do something!"

Why does Sid have to stick his big fat butt into

everything? Zeke thought wearily. He watched Hannah spit on her knee, trying to wash the blood away.

"You give up, freak?" called Sid.

Zeke gritted his teeth. He hated being pushed around like this. He looked back at Otto. The little beast smiled and hopped up and down.

And then Zeke had an idea. It was a wild and crazy whopper of an idea! *Could I really do it?* he wondered. *Will it work?* He didn't know, but he had to try. Hannah was right. He had to do *something!*

CHAPTER 14

Boot It Up

"Time out," called Zeke.

"Ha ha, he needs to change his diapers," yelled Moronica.

"I need to get my lucky soccer shoe," said Zeke.

"Your what?" asked Hannah.

"Be right back," said Zeke, running toward the bushes. As he pushed his way through, he whispered, "Otto! Help!"

Zeke flopped down by the pile of junk they'd brought from home and dug around desperately.

The little beast scampered over.

"What? What?" Otto asked.

"Yeah!" said Zeke, holding up his dad's old combat boot. "Otto, get in here! Quick!"

As Otto dove into the big leather boot, Sid
stuck his head through the bushes. "Trying to
run away, Birdbrain? If you do, I'll make you
sit on this soccer ball till it hatches."

"Just getting my lucky shoe," said Zeke. He kicked off his tennis shoe, then jammed his foot into the huge boot.

"Jeez, what a nimrod," snarled Sid. He turned away in disgust.

"You okay, Otto?" Zeke whispered as he tightened the boot's laces. Otto squirmed around at the front of the boot, trying to get comfortable. Zeke tried not to laugh as Otto's fur tickled his toes.

"Aye, aye, captain," called Otto in a muffled voice.

"All right," said Zeke, "here's the plan…"

CHAPTER 15

Plan B
(Blast the Booger Brains!)

"What are you doing?" asked Hannah.

Zeke stood next to her, wearing the big boot.

"I have a plan," said Zeke.

"A plan to look like a goofball?" asked Hannah.

Sid and Moronica were downfield, laughing, pointing, and making silly faces at Zeke.

"Come on, loser," called Sid. "Come get some!" He smacked a meaty fist into the palm of his other hand.

Nervous sweat popped up on Zeke's forehead. He felt like a bowling ball was rolling around in his belly.

"Gimme the ball," said Zeke through gritted teeth.

Hannah kicked the soccer ball to him. Zeke took a few steps forward, as if he was going to run for the goal. Sid and Moronica rushed at him, whooping and growling.

"Now," said Zeke and kicked the ball with his combat boot. He aimed right at Sid. As Zeke's foot connected with the ball, Otto's little arm shot out of the hole in the boot's toe and smacked the ball. Zeke could barely hear Otto's muttered magic word: "Hoobah!"

POOF!

The soccer ball vanished in a flash of light.

Something else appeared in its place. Something big, with bristly black and white skin. Something with tusks as big as jumbo crayons!

Zeke heard Hannah gasp.

With a snort like rumbling thunder, the pig-monster charged at Sid and Moronica.

"Holy ham hocks!" shouted Sid.

Moronica just stood there, her mouth hanging wide open.

KAPOW! The pig hit them like a runaway steamroller.

The two bullies flew into the air, then tumbled to the ground like big sacks of potatoes.

The pig skidded to a stop, gouging out big grooves in the earth. It turned, pawed the grass, and snorted again. Zeke could swear he saw smoke puffing from the monster's snout.

With a gruesome grunt, the pig charged again. This time it headed right for Zeke!

"Holy cow," cried Zeke. He tried to dodge but the pig was too fast. The monster launched itself like a missile!

This is gonna hurt! thought Zeke.

As the pig slammed into him—

POOF!

The soccer ball was back. It ricocheted off Zeke's stomach and bounced to the ground.

"Hannah…" Zeke wheezed, "make…a goal!"

For a moment, Hannah stood frozen in place, then she raced forward. She kicked the ball. Running past Sid and Moronica, she kicked it again. "Ha ha!" she cried as she booted the ball past the goal line. "I scored! Hooray!"

"That was an awesome swap-o," Zeke muttered to his boot.

"Yay! Me so great," called Otto.

As Hannah walked back, she tossed the ball at Sid and Moronica. "Your turn," she said. "The score is one to eight, you losers!"

"WHAT THE HECK JUST HAPPENED!?" shouted Moronica. She jumped up, rubbing her head. "What did you do, punk?" she yelled at Zeke.

Zeke grinned and shrugged his shoulders.

"Wouldn't you like to know," said Hannah, giggling.

"Weird things happen around that freak," said Sid.

"But there was...I saw..." hollered Moronica. She glared at Zeke. "YOU ARE SO DEAD!"

CHAPTER 16

The Super Swap-0 Surprise!

Sid and Moronica ran forward, kicking the ball back and forth between them.

Zeke sprinted toward them.

"Out of the way!" growled Sid, swinging his beefy arm to block Zeke.

Zeke ducked, then slid in between the bullies like he was sliding toward home plate.

His big boot connected with the ball.

"Hoobah!" cried Otto.

There was a flash of light and a POOF! as the ball sailed up into the air.

"I got it!" cried Sid.

"Me too," called Moronica, running after her cousin.

The ball's a different color, thought Zeke, *but that's all.* He was disappointed.

"Head butt!" Sid called and slammed his head into the ball—
SPLURP!

The ball exploded into goo! Slime splattered over Sid and Moronica. The air filled with the smell of rotten fruit.

Sid yelped, "Holy crud!"

"EEEWWWWWW!" screamed Moronica as she and Sid slipped and slid in the slimy goop.

"Glad I'm not you," said Hannah, snickering loudly.

"Excellent," muttered Zeke.

There was another flash of bright light.

POOF!

Most of the stinky slime disappeared, and the soccer ball was back.

This time Hannah was ready. "Booyah!" she screamed, smashing the ball across the goal line with a mighty kick.

Dancing around like a football player who had just scored a touchdown, Hannah sang out:

"We made a goal, 'cause we're the best!
You big losers failed the test!"

She pointed her finger at Sid.

"I'm cool! I rule! You're just a fool!
You better go to soccer school!"

"This is crazy!" said Moronica, trying to wipe the last of the goop off her face.

"Gimme that, shrimp!" snarled Sid, grabbing the ball from Hannah. Then he shoved her hard. Hannah hit the grass with a THUMP!

"Hey!" cried Zeke.

"You gonna do something about it, Birdbrain?" yelled Sid. He kicked the ball at Zeke as hard as he could.

Without thinking, Zeke dived toward the ball. He spun in midair, and his big boot smacked into the soccer ball. Otto's small hand popped out of the boot and tapped the ball. "Hoobah!"

There was a flash of light...

POOF!

The soccer ball vanished.

There was a thundering BOOM! and a cloud of smelly black smoke. The object that appeared in place of the soccer ball was like a round, black thunderbolt thrown by Zeus. It blasted at Sid like a whistling rocket.

"AAIIIEEE!" Sid squealed and threw himself

flat on the ground. The black iron ball zoomed over his head, then smashed into a tree. The tree blew apart, like it was made of cardboard.

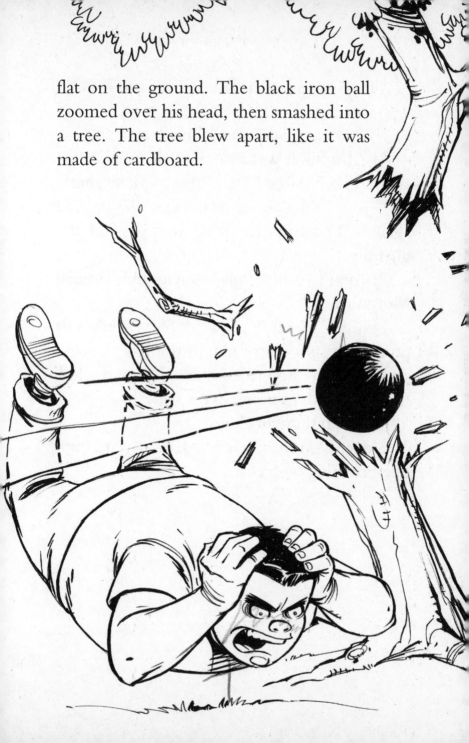

There was another flash of light and POOF! The soccer ball rolled gently to a stop.

"What was that?" gasped Hannah.

"I...I think it was a cannonball," said Zeke.

"Yo ho ho!" said Otto. "From pirate ship!"

"Hey, look," cried Hannah. "We scored again!" The ball was lying just beyond the goal line.

"I don't wanna play anymore," wailed Moronica.

"Forget soccer," growled Sid. "Let's just pound the snot out of him instead!"

Moronica stopped crying. "Sounds like fun," she said, grinning like a shark.

Oh crud, thought Zeke.

Sid and Moronica circled in toward him like prowling wolves.

CHAPTER 17

Double Trouble!

Zeke took off like a rabbit!

"Get him!" yelled Sid.

"Leave him alone," cried Hannah. She jumped on Moronica's back, like a little monkey trying to get a piggyback ride from a gorilla.

"Get off, punk!" screeched Moronica.

Zeke tried to run, but the big combat boot was slowing him down and throwing him off-balance. He had to get to the soccer ball and kick it again. Maybe Otto could swap in another cannonball.

"Don't let him get that ball," shouted Moronica. She tossed Hannah off her back like a wild bronco bucking off a runty cowboy.

"Get ready, Otto!" Zeke made a desperate, lunging kick for the ball—

Just as Sid slammed into him with a flying tackle!

Zeke felt like a charging rhino had smashed into him. The air blasted out of his lungs.

Then everything seemed to happen in slow

motion. Zeke couldn't do anything to stop it. It was like a nightmare.

As Sid plowed into him, Zeke missed the ball completely. His big combat boot snagged on the rough bark of a tall tree and popped off his foot. Otto came tumbling out of the boot, his arm already reaching out for a swap-o. Only the soccer ball wasn't there, the tree was!

"Hoobah!" Otto squeaked. One hand smacked the tree, the other was clinging to the boot's shoelace.

As Sid crash-landed on top of him, Zeke saw two flashes of bright green light!

POOF! The combat boot disappeared. In its place was a brown, goofy-looking frog.

POOF! The tree vanished!

Holy cow! Zeke thought. *Otto did a double swap-o!*

The thing that now stood where the tree had been was gigantic!

Sid was holding Zeke down, unaware of what was happening behind him.

"Get ready to eat a knuckle-sandwich," snarled Sid.

Then Moronica and Hannah screamed.

"Huh?" said Sid.

The earth shook like someone was pounding the ground with a giant hammer. An ear-splitting roar shattered the sky.

"Holy crud," gasped Sid.

No way! thought Zeke, dazed, his brain spinning. *Otto swapped that tree for a—*

"Dude," wailed Sid, "that's a *DINOSAUR!*"

CHAPTER 18

Home Run

There was a flash of pink and polka dots, then SLAM! Zeke and Hannah were knocked to the ground.

"Duck and cover, you yard apes," shouted

Mrs. McQueen. "We got an earthquake!" The old lady lay protectively on top of them.

"I think it's over," called Zeke in a muffled voice.

"All right, pack yer gear," shouted Mrs. McQueen.

Zeke and Hannah tossed everything back in the duffel bag.

Sid stood nearby, his eyes popping, his mouth gasping. He finally managed to shout, "There was a Tyrannosorbus Rox…a Rynnosaurus Tex…there was a DINO!"

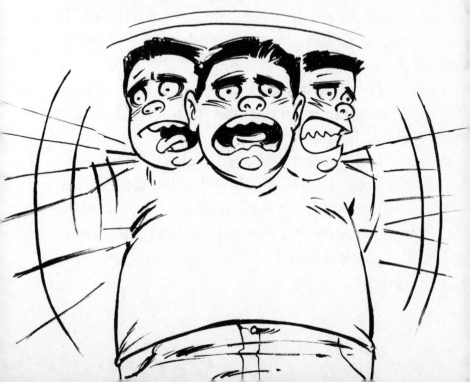

Mrs. McQueen stared at Sid. "Better get home, you walleyed flounder," she ordered. "There's earthquakes lurkin' about."

"We almost lost Otto," Zeke whispered to Hannah.

"Who in the whalin' waterspout is Otto?" asked Mrs. McQueen, whirling around.

"That's our...uh...soccer ball," Hannah said.

Zeke hid the backpack behind him.

"Stow the chatter," yelled Miss McQueen. "Statues are jumpin' into trees! Bananas are fallin' from the sky! We gotta vamoose." She hurriedly tossed Zeke, Hannah, and the duffel bag over her shoulders and hauled them to the car.

Three minutes later, the purple station wagon screeched to a stop in front of Zeke and Hannah's house.

The old lady grabbed Zeke, Hannah, and the bulky bag, ran up the sidewalk, kicked open the front door, tossed everything onto the living room couch, and shouted, "My watch is over!"

"Back already?" Mom asked from the other room.

"It was a close one," Miss McQueen said. She winked at Zeke and Hannah, then marched out.

In the distance, Zeke could hear the whooping sirens of fire trucks and police cars heading for the park.

"What's all the commotion?" muttered Zeke's mom, turning on the TV.

"Uh oh," said Zeke. "Come on!" He grabbed the lumpy duffel bag and dragged it up the stairs and into his room.

Hannah snatched up the backpack and ran after him.

Closing the door behind her, Hannah unzipped the backpack. Otto leaped out of the pack, crawled under Zeke's bed, and dragged out a bag of pretzels. "Snackies!"

Hannah flopped down on the bed. "I can't believe I lost my golden egg," she said with a loud sigh.

"I can't believe I almost hit Sid with a cannonball," said Zeke, grinning. His smile faded. "Yeah, sorry we didn't get your egg back."

"But we saved Otto," said Hannah.

"Me was froggy food," Otto said, crunching a pretzel.

Hannah sat up and smiled. "Hey! Otto can swap my egg back!"

"No way!" Zeke said. "Swap-o is too dangerous. Flying cannonballs! Killer bananas! And we almost got chomped by a dinosaur!"

"Come on," Hannah begged. "We also beat Sid and his goony cousin. We invented a new game."

"Yay," said Otto. "Swap-o ball!"

"That was kind of fun," Zeke said, "now that it's over."

Hannah leaped off the bed and grabbed a few of Zeke's toys. "Get ready, Otto. I'll toss them at you and you swap-o them."

"Hang on," Zeke yelled. "If we're going to do this, we'll do it right. Like scientists."

"I'll get the ruler," Hannah giggled.

"Me get a cookie," Otto said with a snort.

"Let's start with swapping something small," Zeke said, searching his desk. "Small and *safe*. A-ha! How about this postage stamp from the letter Dad sent? It has a picture of a happy koala bear on it."

"Do it," Hannah cheered.

"Okay, Otto," Zeke said, holding out the postage stamp. "Nothing with fangs!"

"Yo ho," said Otto. "Hope me eats it before it eats me." The little beast tapped the stamp and shouted, "Hoobah!"

ABOUT THE AUTHORS

Nate Evans has illustrated over thirty-five books and written a few more, including several picture books coauthored with Laura Numeroff. The latest of these is the *New York Times* bestseller *The Jellybeans and the Big Book Bonanza*. Nate currently lives in Georgia with his wonderful wife and three goofy dogs.

Vince Evans started his artistic training by copying his big brother Nate's drawings. Vince has worked for numerous comic and book companies, and he has won the Spectrum Silver Award for excellence in comic art.